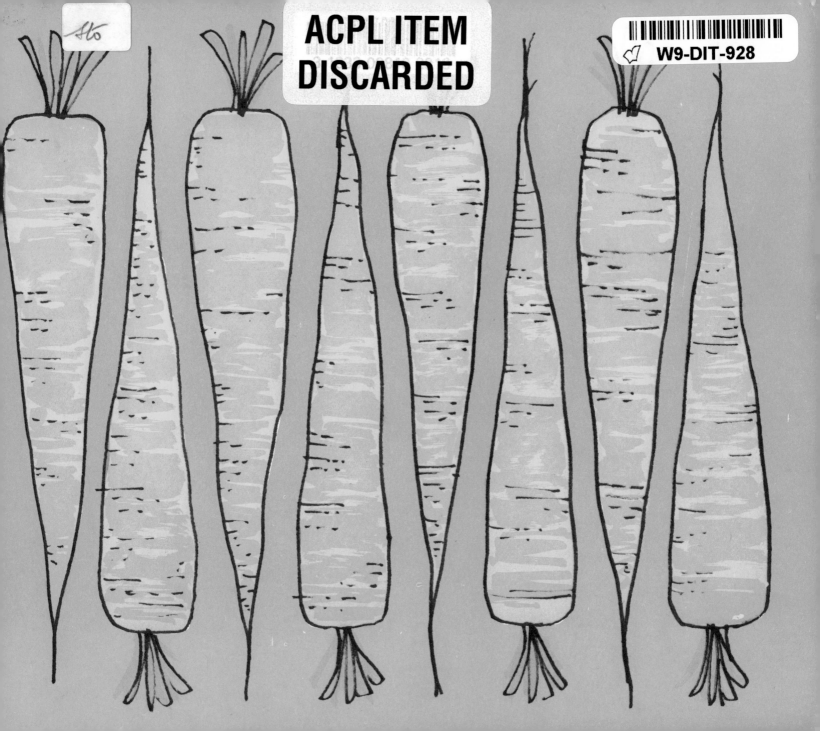

Bunny in the Honeysuckle Patch

by Jane Thayer or Pseud.

Catherine Wooley

PICTURES BY SEYMOUR FLEISHMAN

WILLIAM MORROW AND COMPANY • NEW YORK 1965

A BABY BUNNY lived with his mother
under a sweet-smelling honeysuckle patch.
The honeysuckle grew near an old house where nobody lived.

Only the hummingbird and the bee,
who came to drink the honey in the honeysuckle,
knew the baby bunny lived there.
He was safe and snug!
"You are my little honey bunny," Mother Bunny told him.

Then Miss Cobble moved into the old house.

First Miss Cobble found a farmer with a plow.

"Please plow the garden," she said.

"Now that I live in the country,

I'm going to grow peas, beans, carrots,

squash and tender green lettuce.

I'm going to have lovely fresh vegetables to eat."

"We are going to have

fresh carrots and tender green lettuce too, honey bunny,"

Mother Bunny whispered with a bunny chuckle.

Then Miss Cobble came out

with her garden shears and her spade.

"Look at all this honeysuckle!" she said.

"It is running wild.

I'm going to dig it out and plant petunias here."

Mother Bunny was away from home.

Baby Bunny, all alone in the honeysuckle, was frightened.

He hoped Miss Cobble wouldn't dig him out, too.

Miss Cobble dug away at the honeysuckle roots.

She stopped to rest,

and just then Mother Bunny

came hopping happily home across the lawn.

Miss Cobble saw her.

There is a rabbit!

He will eat up my lovely fresh peas, beans, carrots,
squash and tender green lettuce,
when they begin to grow, she thought.
"Shoo!" shouted Miss Cobble.
She chased Mother Bunny
out of the yard, *shoo, shoo, shoo*.
Then she went back
to digging honeysuckle.

Baby Bunny's heart was hammering under the vines.
But the roots were so long and tough
that Miss Cobble found it hard work.
"I've dug enough for today," she said.
Baby Bunny sighed with relief.

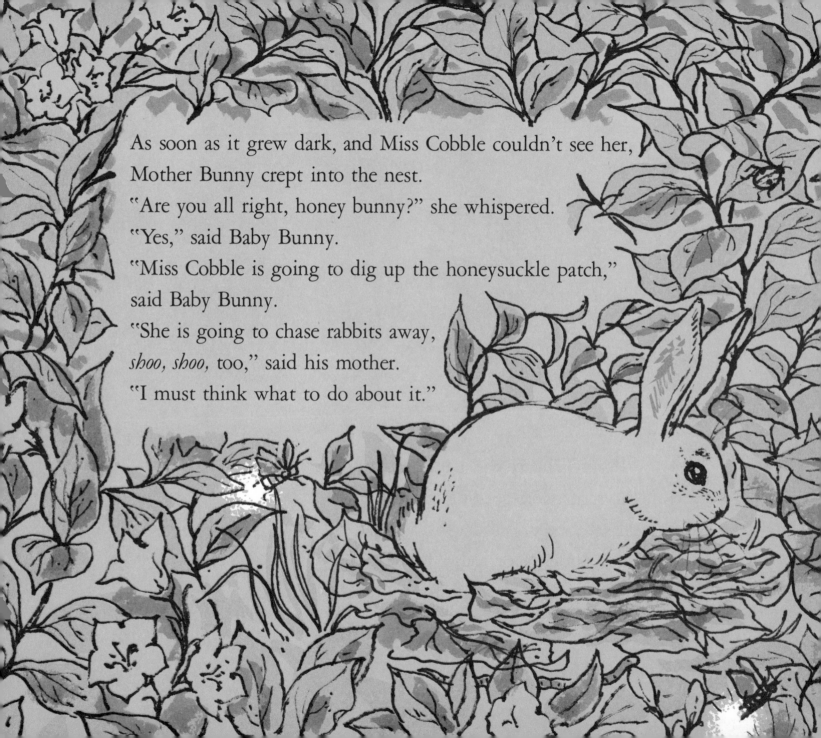

As soon as it grew dark, and Miss Cobble couldn't see her,
Mother Bunny crept into the nest.

"Are you all right, honey bunny?" she whispered.

"Yes," said Baby Bunny.

"Miss Cobble is going to dig up the honeysuckle patch,"
said Baby Bunny.

"She is going to chase rabbits away,
shoo, shoo, too," said his mother.

"I must think what to do about it."

As the days passed,

Miss Cobble dug away at the honeysuckle patch.

She came closer and closer to the bunnies' nest.

Baby Bunny kept very still,

but he trembled under the vines.

At last Mother Bunny said, "I must get some advice.

I'll ask my friend Daniel the dog,

across the road, what he would do."

She asked Daniel the dog,

"What would *you* do

if Miss Cobble was digging up your honeysuckle patch

and chased you *shoo, shoo* away?"

"I would bite her," said Daniel the dog savagely.

"That's what I'd do. Shall I bite her for you?"

"If you would, please," said the gentle Mother Bunny.

Mother Bunny watched from the woods.
Miss Cobble came out.
"Hello, Daniel," she said, "here's a bone for you."
Did Daniel the dog bite her?
He did not.
He ate up the bone and wagged his tail for more.
Miss Cobble dug up
some more honeysuckle roots.

"That didn't work," said Mother Bunny sadly.
"I'll ask my friend Claribel the cat,
up on the hill, what she would do."
She asked Claribel, up on the hill,
"What would *you* do
if Miss Cobble was digging up
your honeysuckle patch
and chased you *shoo, shoo* away?"

"I would scratch her,"
said Claribel fiercely.
"I certainly would.
Shall I scratch her for you?"
"Yes, please,"
said the timid Mother Bunny.

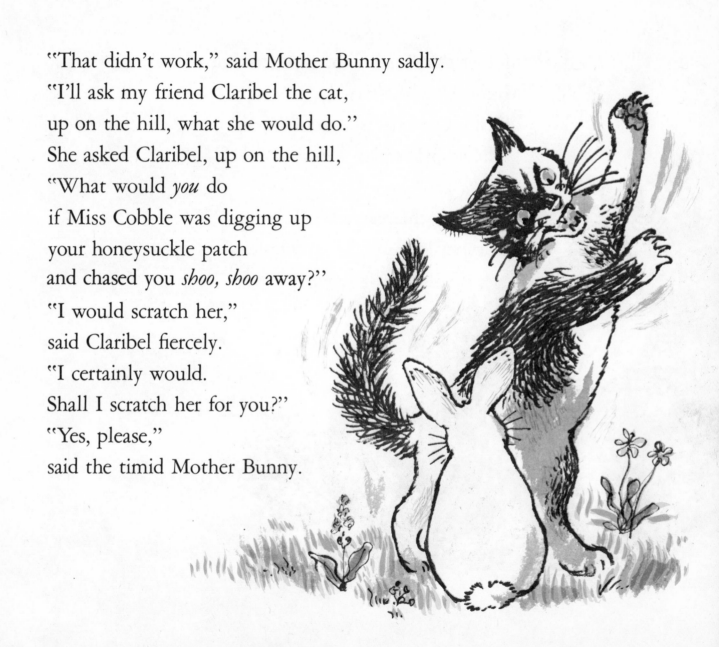

Mother Bunny watched from behind a bush.

Miss Cobble came out.

"Hello, Claribel," she said. "Here's some fish for you."

Did Claribel scratch her?

She *did not*.

She ate up the fish

and rubbed against Miss Cobble's legs, purring.

Miss Cobble dug up more honeysuckle.
She chased Mother Bunny out of the yard
every time she saw her.
Mother Bunny thought,
I'll ask my friend Freddy the field mouse
what he would do.
She asked Freddy the field mouse,
"What would *you* do
if Miss Cobble was digging up your honeysuckle patch
and chased you *shoo, shoo* away?"
"I'd scare her," said Freddy boldly.
"Yes, ma'am!
I'd slip into that house and scare her half to death.
Shall I scare her half to death for you?"
"Thank you," said the helpless Mother Bunny.

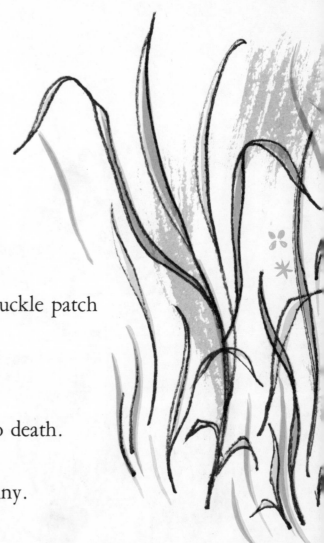

Freddy the field mouse
slipped into the house
and made all the noise he could.
Miss Cobble said
it sounded quite friendly,
hearing Freddy around.

She dug up a lot more honeysuckle.
"There is no one else," said Mother Bunny in despair.
"I shall have to take my little honey bunny
out of his safe, snug nest into the cold, strange world.
Tomorrow we will go."

Early the next morning,
when the sun was just peeping over the trees
and the grass sparkled with dew,
Mother Bunny said, "Come on, bunny honey.
We can't wait any longer.
Today Miss Cobble is sure to uncover our nest."
Mother Bunny and Baby Bunny came out of the honeysuckle.
They did not see a crouching figure lurking behind a bush.
It was a cat—not Claribel, their friend—
but a strange black cat with fierce, gleaming eyes.
Mother Bunny and Baby Bunny
started across the lawn toward the woods.

The strange cat with gleaming eyes crept around the bush.
Mother Bunny saw him.
She was so frightened that she gave seven giant leaps
and disappeared into the woods.
Baby Bunny was so frightened
that he did not give one small leap.
He stayed where he was,
his little heart hammering with fear.
The strange cat fixed Baby Bunny
with his fierce, gleaming eyes.
He crept closer and closer.
Baby Bunny was too terrified
to move.

Suddenly the door of the house opened.
Out came Miss Cobble, extra early,
with her garden shears and her spade.
Miss Cobble saw the strange cat creeping.
"Shoo!" she cried.
The strange cat ran away.

Miss Cobble looked to see what the cat had been after.
She couldn't believe her eyes
when she looked down and saw a baby bunny.

"Oh!" exclaimed Miss Cobble.
"You little honey bunny!"
Then she suddenly cried,
"Is that your mother I've been chasing away?
I didn't know she was a mother bunny!
You poor Baby Bunny.
Wait, I'll get you a carrot."

Miss Cobble threw down her shears and her spade.

She brought Baby Bunny a carrot.

"I suppose you live in the honeysuckle," she said thoughtfully.

"Well, I'll leave the rest of it.

You can stay here, where you are safe,

until you are grown up."

She gently put Baby Bunny back in the honeysuckle patch,

and her shears and spade in the barn.

After dark Mother Bunny came back to the nest.

"Come on, bunny honey," she whispered.

"The strange cat has gone,
and Miss Cobble can't see us now."

"She said we didn't have to go away," said Baby Bunny.

"*What* did she say?" said his astonished mother.

"She said I was a honey bunny," said Baby Bunny.

"She gave me this carrot."

"Well!" said Mother Bunny.

Then Mother Bunny looked proudly
at her baby bunny.

And she gave a bunny chuckle.

"You always *were* a honey bunny,"
she said.

After that Miss Cobble gave them a carrot a day.
And she never dug up the rest of the honeysuckle patch,
on account of the hummingbird, the bee, and baby bunnies.

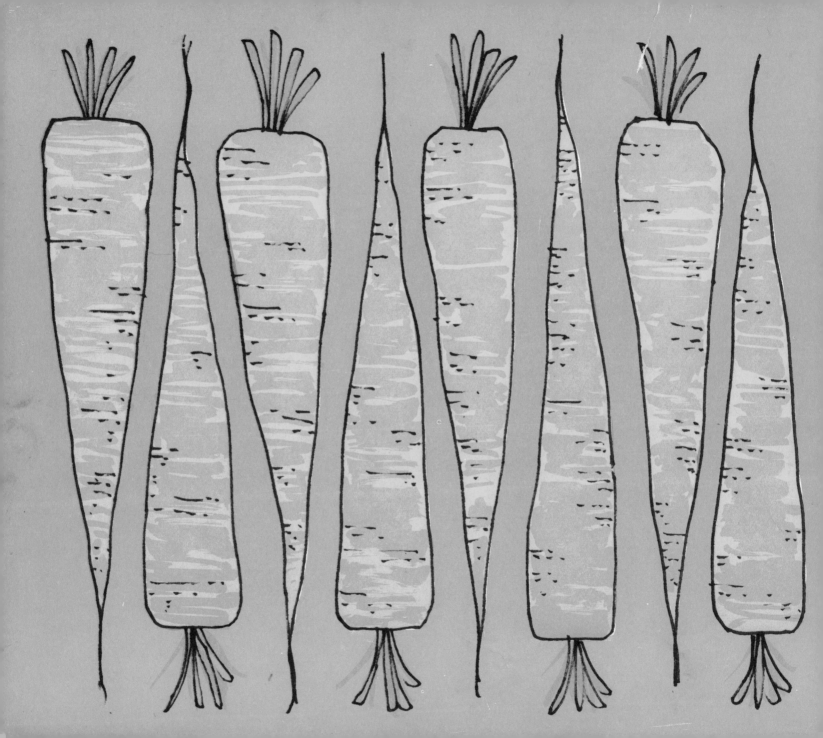